MICHAEL Q.

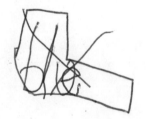 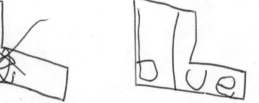

blue

Erin Quinn

A Lucas/Spielberg Presentation

THE LAND BEFORE TIME

A Don Bluth Film

Adapted by **Jim Razzi**

From a Story by
Judy Freudberg & Tony Geiss

Screenplay by **Stu Krieger**

Illustrated by
David Kirschner and **Beverly Lazor-Bahr**

Book Design by **Deborah Bethel Ferranti**

PUBLISHERS • **GROSSET & DUNLAP** • **NEW YORK**

Exclusively yours from JCPenney

1 The Birth of Littlefoot

One night, long, long ago, three huge figures stood in a gentle rain, waiting patiently by a lonely nest. Raindrops splashed against cracked and smashed eggshells, which glistened when a bolt of lightning zigzagged across the sky. Only one egg was still whole, and the three long-necks were guarding it.

As the two older, wrinkled long-necks looked on, their daughter nudged her egg gently with her nose. It was taking such a long time to hatch that she was worried. Suddenly it bounced and rocked, and the two older long-necks smiled.

But the egg didn't break open.

"It is a hard birth," murmured its mother.

As if in agreement, a flash of lightning cracked across the sky and a crash of thunder shook the air. The egg bounced again...and again. Then it lurched clear out of the nest, rolled down the sloping mound that surrounded the nest, and wobbled to a stop by a shallow pond.

Suddenly a hungry claw-hand leapt out of the nearby bushes. He grabbed the egg greedily and sped off. He was fast, but the mother

long-neck was faster. With one swipe of her strong neck she knocked the claw-hand to the ground, and the egg flew out of his hands. The claw-hand scurried away, angry at being cheated out of his dinner.

But now the egg rolled crazily down a steep hill. Mother long-neck watched helplessly as it went over branches and rocks and finally plopped into a swift, shallow stream.

"Oh, no!" she said, gasping. "The falls!"

The egg suddenly went over the edge of a steep waterfall and disappeared into the foaming water. It bobbed up at the bottom of the falls, spinning and rolling furiously in the whirlpools. The rushing water slammed it against a bed of soft sand by the edge of the stream. The egg rocked to a stop and lay there, totally still.

The long-necks rushed over to it. In despair the mother nudged the egg once more. "Is the last egg dead now, too?" she thought.

Suddenly a loud *CRACK!* made her pull back from the egg in surprise. There was still a chance!

The three long-necks watched in awe as a wagging tail popped out, sending pieces of shell flying through the air. The tail was followed by two sturdy hind legs that wiggled their way out. Finally a cute little head appeared. It was a perfect baby boy long-neck!

The little baby looked around, bewildered. His mother cooed at him gently and he looked up. As she lowered her head, he shied away. She just unfurled her huge tongue and gave him a loving lick. Suddenly the world was a fine place.

"Why, he's just adorable!" said grandmother long-neck. "What will you call him?"

The mother took her baby lovingly in her mouth and swung him high in the air and onto her back. The baby snuggled warmly against her neck, making a bleating sound remarkably like "Mama."

"I will call him Littlefoot," she said.

"Littlefoot," echoed grandfather long-neck, nodding his head, "a good name."

A curious bunch of small animals had surrounded the proud mother and grandparents and were also nodding to each other in approval. As far as any of them knew, this baby would be the last long-neck born in the area, and they looked up at him with interest.

"Yes," they said, whispering and gossiping with each other. "It is a good name for the last long-neck—Littlefoot!"

2 "Three-horns Don't Play with Long-necks!"

As Littlefoot grew into a strong, handsome young long-neck, his mother and grandparents were very proud of him. Life had been easy for a while, but the land was changing. Every day it seemed as if there were fewer leaves on the trees.

"Will it always be like this?" asked Littlefoot as he chewed on some bad-tasting pine needles.

"No, dear," answered his mother. "That is why we have been traveling. All the herds are following the bright circle in the sky to the place where it touches the ground. It will lead us to the Great Valley."

At that moment Littlefoot's mother looked up and gasped with delight. "Littlefoot, look! A tree star!"

She reached up and gently plucked the last star-shaped leaf from a tall tree. She placed it next to Littlefoot and he looked at it admiringly.

"The Great Valley is filled with green-food like this," said his mother, "and fresh cool water. It is a wonderful place, where we can all live happily together."

"When will we get there?" asked Littlefoot impatiently.

"I—I don't know," answered his mother. "But if we have faith and follow the bright circle to where it touches the ground, we will get there."

"Have *you* ever been there?" asked Littlefoot.

Smiling gently, his mother answered no.

"Well…how can you be sure it's really there?" asked Littlefoot.

"Some things you see with your eyes. Others you see with your heart," answered his mother.

"I don't understand, Mother," Littlefoot said.

"Someday perhaps you will."

Littlefoot looked down at the tree star. He was about to take a bite when he heard someone yell.

He poked his head through some reeds and saw a little girl three-horn charging about, butting everything and everyone in sight and yelling.

Littlefoot laughed in delight. He came out of his hiding place in the reeds. The little three-horn took one look at him and smiled.

All of a sudden she yelled, "Arrrgh!" She was going to charge *him!*

"What a great game," thought Littlefoot as he charged the little three-horn.

Suddenly a huge, stern-looking three-horn blocked his way. It was the little three-horn's father. He scowled at Littlefoot and then turned to his child. "Come, Cera," he said. "Three-horns never play with long-necks!"

The little three-horn seemed to change. She looked as if she wanted to attack Littlefoot for real.

Littlefoot tripped over his own tail as he tried to back away. His mother came to the rescue just in time and plucked him up by the tail. Cera's father did the same to her.

Littlefoot scrambled up near his mother's head. "What's a long-neck?" he asked.

"Why, that's what *we* are, dear," his mother answered.

9

Littlefoot said, "Oh," and thought about it. Then he asked, "Why can't I play with that three-horn?"

"Questions, questions," said his mother, sighing. "It's just the way it is. We all keep to ourselves…the three-horns, the spike-tails, the swimmers, the fliers….We never do anything together."

"But—" said Littlefoot.

His mother cut in. "When we reach the Great Valley, you will have many of your own kind to play with."

Littlefoot still didn't understand. He wondered if they ever really *would* reach the Great Valley. He was still thinking about this while the family rested in a shady glen near a swamp. As he lay down by his mother, he put the tree star underneath his head as a pillow.

He had no sooner fallen asleep than he heard a funny noise. *Ribbet, ribbet!* He lazily opened one eye. A great big hopper was staring him right in the face. The hopper leapt away, and Littlefoot jumped up and followed it.

Suddenly a voice said, "That's my hopper!" It was the little three-horn, Cera.

Littlefoot said, "I saw him first."

"But he's in my pond," Cera yelled back. She chased the creature down a muddy slope, bumping right into it. With a *ribbet* and a *plop*, it disappeared into a swampy pond.

Then Littlefoot slid down and bumped into Cera. He thought she would get mad, but she just splashed after the hopper, which was making bubbles on the surface of the murky brown water.

Cera giggled with delight and jumped on the bubbles, popping each one as it came up. Littlefoot joined in, and soon the two of them were playing as if their fight a short while ago had never happened. They were so busy playing that they didn't see a dark shadow growing bigger and bigger. Suddenly a terrifying roar filled the air, and the ground shook under their feet.

They both looked up and saw an enormous figure heading toward them. Their hearts froze in terror!

3 Sharptooth!

Littlefoot and Cera stood in the shadow of the most ferocious and deadly creature in the land—Sharptooth!

"What'll we do?" screamed Cera.

"Quick!" yelled Littlefoot. "Into that tree!"

They both dove into a huge hollow tree. But the monster saw them. With a mighty roar, he crushed the tree between his terrible jaws.

Splinters of dry branches and chunks of dead bark rained on Littlefoot and Cera as they slid into the swamp mud.

"What now?" cried Littlefoot.

Cera looked around in panic. Then she spotted an opening in a thicket. "In there!" she yelled.

Sharptooth was at their heels, and they could feel the ground tremble. Littlefoot and Cera cowered in the center of the brambles, thinking they were safe, but Sharptooth chewed and ripped through the twisted boughs. Littlefoot could feel the monster's hot breath on his tail. Leaping up to get away, he got caught in some thorny black

branches. Sharptooth bore down on him with evil glee.

At the very last moment Littlefoot freed himself. One of the hard thorny branches snapped back and hit Sharptooth right in the eye. The monster bellowed in pain and reared back from the brambles. Then, with a terrible fury, he plunged back into the thicket, searching for the puny creature that had dared to injure him.

Littlefoot and Cera watched fearfully as the giant creature suddenly stopped and sniffed the air. Then he stomped out of their view.

"Let's move further back," said Cera.

"No, wait," warned Littlefoot. But it was too late. "Hey, wait for me!" he yelled as he ran after her.

Littlefoot's cry gave away their hiding place, and with an angry growl, Sharptooth attacked the bushes once more. They were trapped!

Closer and closer the monster came. Although one of his eyes was swollen shut, he was growling softly, enjoying his moment of revenge. Then he opened his jaws and pounced.

Suddenly, from out of nowhere, a huge tail slammed into his head and snapped it around. It was Littlefoot's mother!

Sharptooth shook his head to clear it. Then he turned to face his attacker. When he saw Littlefoot's mother, he bolted up and started to pace around her. With a speed that was surprising for such a heavy animal, Sharptooth lunged at Littlefoot's mother.

"Run, Littlefoot!" she yelled as she avoided the attack. Cera and Littlefoot tried to get away but found themselves underneath her feet.

The huge monster attacked again and snapped his jaws, hoping for a quick kill. But Littlefoot's mother sidestepped the attack again and gave the monster another powerful blow with her strong tail. Sharptooth reeled back dizzily but quickly regained his balance. He jumped on Littlefoot's mother and held on savagely, trying to bite her neck. But she twisted and squirmed and fought back.

Littlefoot and Cera cringed against the wall of a cliff, watching the battle with mounting terror.

"Run, now!" cried Littlefoot's mother. "I will follow you."

The young long-neck and three-horn ran as fast as they could, looking back in fright. Littlefoot's mother had now freed herself from Sharptooth's death grip and was crashing through rocks and boulders, trying to make a path for them to escape.

Once again the beast charged, and once again Littlefoot's mother struck him down. His fall sent a huge wave of mud toward Littlefoot and Cera, which caught them up and carried them right into the jaws of the raging monster. Littlefoot's mother, realizing that she would have to act swiftly to save the two youngsters, bravely leapt forward and hit Sharptooth in the belly with all her might. The great beast went down with a ground-shaking force.

"Now, Littlefoot," cried his mother, "run through that canyon!"

Littlefoot and Cera scooted through a small canyon between the cliff walls. Littlefoot's mother was right behind them as Sharptooth scrambled to his feet. Just as Cera and Littlefoot found shelter among some rocks, the ground suddenly began to move. A crack appeared and rapidly began to widen. The ground underneath them rumbled and shook and tilted sideways. Rocks, trees, and chunks of earth exploded into the air as they clung to each other, trying to stay on their feet.

Littlefoot's mother was nowhere to be seen. Only Sharptooth was still there, stomping their way with a wild look on his face.

Littlefoot realized that Sharptooth was no longer chasing them but only trying to save his own life.

Suddenly the ground they were standing on tilted wildly, and amid a spray of hot steam and black smoke, the two youngsters slid back, right onto Sharptooth's toes!

Now the three of them were stepping back together. A deep canyon had opened, and they were all sliding toward it! Sharptooth was going tail first, so Littlefoot and Cera scrambled up his body to his head.

Even in his terror, the huge beast saw his chance to crush the tiny creatures who had caused him so much trouble. But as his jaws opened wide for the kill, the snap of a familiar tail sent Sharptooth flipping in the air. Littlefoot and Cera went sailing up past him. The next moment, the huge beast fell screeching into the dark canyon, slipping and clawing at the sides. A few heartbeats later Littlefoot and Cera screamed as they slipped down after him.

4 Alone and Afraid

Littlefoot and Cera were suddenly snatched up in midair by Littlefoot's mother. But they were safe only for a moment, because other cracks appeared in the ground and the earth continued to rip apart.

As Cera ran off to find her family, Littlefoot tried to stay close to his mother. But the steam gushing up from the jagged cracks in the ground, the noise, and the tumbling rocks terrified the herds. They crashed into each other, and stumbled and fell, trying to escape the terrible earthquake. In the confusion, Littlefoot lost sight of his mother and found himself alone and frightened.

The earthquake was coming to an end. With a few more bursts of smoke and steam and a final shudder, the ground stopped trembling. As rain began to fall, Littlefoot vainly searched for his mother.

"Mother? Mother...where are you?" he cried.

Only the echo of his own voice came back to him. Then, beyond a huge boulder, he saw her on the cracked and smoking ground. She was lying on her side, breathing with deep wheezing gasps.

"Mother, what's wrong?" cried Littlefoot. "Get up!"

His mother struggled to rise, but she was too weak. Sharptooth had wounded her after all.

"Mother, please get up," pleaded Littlefoot.

She tried again, but once more fell back. She looked at Littlefoot in great pity. She knew that it was the end for her. She hoped with all her heart that Littlefoot would be brave and go on without her.

"Dear Littlefoot," she whispered, "do you remember…the way to the Great Valley?"

"I guess so," answered Littlefoot. "But why do I have to know? You're going to be with me."

"Yes, Littlefoot, that's right," said his mother. "I'll be with you all the way to the Great Valley even if you can't see me."

"That's silly. I can always see you," cried Littlefoot.

His mother smiled at him gently. "I'll be in your heart, Littlefoot," she said. "Let your heart guide you—it whispers, so listen carefully."

His mother looked as if she were about to get up again, but she only raised her head and gazed into the distance. Then she lowered her long neck to the ground and was very still.

"Mother?" whispered Littlefoot, drawing close to her. "Mother?" But she did not answer. Littlefoot turned and walked away into the driving rain.

At the top of a steep sand hill Littlefoot stood with tears in his eyes. Making his way down the hill, he lost his balance and tumbled to the bottom, landing on an odd-looking spiked rock.

"Hey!" the rock yelled. "Watch where you're falling!" Littlefoot was so surprised that he fell off. Then he realized that the rock was a big old spiked turtle.

The turtle came over and sniffed at him. "My, my, my..." he said, "you thinkin' about startin' a river? What's the trouble? You can tell old Rooter."

"It's not fair!" Littlefoot wailed. "She should have known better. She knew Sharptooth was dangerous. It's all my mother's fault. What am I going to do without her?"

Rooter looked at him kindly. "Oh, I see...I see."

"Why did I wander so far from home? If I hadn't, we would have never met Sharptooth."

"It was not your fault," Rooter said gently. "It was not your mother's fault. Now, you pay attention to old Rooter. It is nobody's fault. The great circle of life has a beginning. But you see, not all of us arrive together at the end."

"But what will I do? I miss her so much."

"And you will always miss her," Rooter answered. "But she will always be with you, as long as you remember what she taught you."

"My tummy hurts," Littlefoot said with despair in his voice.

"That, too, will go in time," murmured Rooter. Then he snorted and lumbered away.

The long-neck was alone once more. He looked up, ready to cry again. But his eye caught something green and shimmering, floating on the wind. He brushed away a tear to see better. It was the tree star his mother had given him. It hovered over his head, then floated to the ground, surrounding him with a warm, glowing light that made him feel good all over.

He looked up at the sky once more. He saw a big cloud shaped just like his mother, and the wind in the rocks and trees formed themselves into words.

"Dear Littlefoot," they murmured, "do you remember the way to the Great Valley?"

Littlefoot's heart swelled with joy. Rooter was right—his mother was still with him. They were bound together with a love that was stronger than death.

"Remember," continued the whispering voice, "follow the bright circle past the great rock that looks like a long-neck…and past the mountains that burn. And I'll be with you, even though you cannot see me. I'll be in your heart, Littlefoot. Let your heart guide you.…Remember…it whispers."

Littlefoot placed the tree star on his head. He knew that he wasn't really alone. With his head high, he marched on across the shattered landscape.

A short while later, he saw someone up ahead. It was the little three-horn, Cera! He rushed up to her.

"Hello!" he cried, glad to see her.

"What do *you* want?" snapped Cera.

Littlefoot was puzzled. Was she still angry with him?

"I—I don't know," he stammered. "Where are you going?"

"I'm going to find my own kind," she answered. "They're on the other side of this canyon."

"But you can't get to the other side from here," said Littlefoot.

Cera said, "Maybe *you* can't." Then she started down the steep side of the canyon.

"Wait!" cried Littlefoot. "I'm going to the Great Valley. We could help each other."

Cera was about to say that she didn't need any help, when she slipped down into the darkness of the canyon.

For a moment Littlefoot was tempted to follow. It was better than being alone, he thought.

But he didn't. He could hear Cera shouting up to him, "I'm going to find my sisters.…"

Littlefoot turned sadly and walked toward the setting sun. Even with the tree star to comfort him, he started to cry again.

He hadn't gone far when he came to a small pond. In its clear surface he saw his own tearful face staring back at him. Suddenly his face broke into a thousand pieces as the water erupted in front of him.

5 Littlefoot Finds Friends

Out of the pond popped a little female big-mouth, younger than Littlefoot and friendly looking. "Hello," said the little big-mouth. "My name's Ducky. What's yours?"

Littlefoot sniffed back his tears and ignored her.

"I said hello," said Ducky. "Can't you talk, huh?"

Littlefoot remembered how Cera had acted toward him. He said, "Long-necks don't talk to...whatever you are."

Ducky couldn't understand. "I'm a long-neck like you," she finally answered. "See?" She stretched her neck to make it as long as she could.

Littlefoot just shook his head and stared at her, as he thought Cera would do. Ducky shrank back and looked sad.

"All right. I am not a long-neck," she cried. "I am a big-mouth. But I am alone. Yep, I am. I lost my family in the big earthshake."

Littlefoot's heart filled with pity. He didn't like pretending to be something he was not. He no longer cared what Cera would do.

"Do you want to go with me?" he asked.

"Oh, yes, I do!" cried Ducky, jumping up and down with joy.

"Come on then," said Littlefoot. "But you'll have to keep up."

"I will keep up," answered Ducky. "Where are we going? Huh?"

"To the Great Valley," said Littlefoot. "I'm not going to stop until I find my grandparents."

"Oh, goody," cried Ducky. "Maybe I will find my family there, too."

Littlefoot just nodded and walked off in the direction of the bright circle in the sky. Ducky skipped and bounced alongside, trying to keep up. She soon made a game of it and giggled in delight.

The next day Littlefoot and Ducky crossed a dry lake bed. They were both very hungry, but there was nothing to eat except straggly

palm trees. Littlefoot bit down on one and heard a strange squeak.

"The tree is talking," cried Ducky.

"No, it isn't," mumbled Littlefoot.

Suddenly a small creature slid down, right onto his face! Something fluttered and squawked around his head and he let go of the tree with a cry. The squawking thing scrambled away and scurried into a nearby hole. Littlefoot and Ducky peered in and came face to face with a sorry-looking little flier.

"Who are you?" asked Ducky.

The little flier gave out a whistling sound and said, "My name is Petrie." He smiled at them.

"Did I flied off the tree?" he asked hopefully.

"No, you fell," answered Ducky.

Petrie gave out a series of sad whistles. "I no flied. I falled."

"But if you can't fly, how did you get up that tree?" asked Ducky.

"I climb," answered the littler flier.

"Fliers aren't supposed to climb," said Littlefoot. "They're supposed to fly."

Petrie whistled again and said, "Too hard to fly."

Petrie soon made friends with Littlefoot and Ducky and asked if he could go with them to the Great Valley. Littlefoot felt sorry for the little creature and didn't want to leave him all alone, so he said yes.

In the meantime Cera was alone in the deep canyon. She wandered along, jumping at every sound and shadow. She missed Littlefoot—even if he was a long-neck. Clouds had covered the sun, sending the canyon into darkness. Cera bumped into something and bounced back.

"What was that?" she said aloud.

As clouds moved away and shafts of sunlight streamed down, she could see that she had bumped into Sharptooth!

Cera started to bolt, when she noticed that his good eye was closed and he wasn't moving. He was dead, she guessed. That made

her braver. She charged at the huge head and gave her battle cry, "Arrrghhh!"

She stopped just short of butting it, then backed up and charged again. She backed up a third time and dug her feet into the ground, lowered her head, and charged. Just as she was about to hit the monster's head, she glanced up and cried in fright—Sharptooth's eye was open and glaring at her hatefully. He was still alive!

Cera screamed and scrambled up the canyon side. But Sharptooth's tail slammed down in front of her. It looked as if she was trapped!

As darkness fell Littlefoot, Ducky, and Petrie were plodding along a bleak, dried-up plain. Petrie tried to keep up with his two new friends, but his little legs couldn't do it. He climbed up to Littlefoot's head, rolled up the tree star that Littlefoot still carried, and tucked it under his wing.

"This much better," he said with a sigh.

Littlefoot shook his head. "I'm not a carrier," he said. "Get off! You're a flier, so start flying." But Petrie wouldn't budge. "Then I'll make you fly," said Littlefoot.

With the little flier clinging to his head, he started to run. Petrie

flapped his wings in the wind. But he was too scared to let go.

Suddenly a terrible scream echoed down the plain. The three friends stopped in their tracks. The screaming came nearer and nearer. In the darkness the three travelers stumbled into the skeleton of a large animal. They all turned to run the other way, but it was too late. With a wild rush, the screaming creature ran into their midst.

6   False Hopes

The moon suddenly came out from behind a cloud, and Littlefoot could now see that the screaming creature was Cera!

"Cera, what happened?" he yelled. "Why are you so frightened?"

"Frightened? Me? Why are *you* so frightened!"

"W-we're not," Littlefoot stammered.

"Well, you should be frightened," Cera continued. "I've just met Sharptooth, and he's alive!"

"That's impossible," Littlefoot said. "Sharptooth is dead."

Cera stamped her feet. "He's alive. I saw him. His one big eye was looking at me. I fought him bravely and just barely escaped."

Littlefoot didn't believe her story, but he admired her courage. "Would you like to join us?" he asked.

"Why not?" Cera said with a shrug. "You will need a brave three-horn with you."

The next morning the four of them trudged on across the barren land. When the bright circle was high in the sky, Ducky came upon a nest with one unhatched egg lying among broken shells. Strange sounds were coming from the egg—snoring, then yawning. Ducky gave a cry of delight and tapped the egg. It started to crack open. A sleepy head appeared. Ducky quickly peeled away the rest of the shell, and there stood a sleepy-eyed spike-tail.

"You are a spike-tail, so I will call you Spike," Ducky said.

The rest of the group came running up. "This is my new friend, Spike," said Ducky. "Can we take him with us? Huh? Huh?"

"He'll slow us down," Cera said. "All spike-tails can do is eat and burp. Sharptooth will catch up and eat *us!*"

"No more dumb stories," Littlefoot said sternly.

"I'm telling the truth!" Cera cried.

Over Cera's protests Spike joined the group. As they were

crossing a barren valley Littlefoot found a brook trickling up through the parched ground. He sniffed the air. "I smell tree stars!" he cried.

Littlefoot raised his neck and peered through an opening between some huge boulders. In the valley below was a cluster of beautiful green trees! When he told the others about it, everyone started to talk at once.

"The Great Valley!" Ducky cried.

"Yes, the Great Valley," echoed Cera.

"But wait," said Littlefoot. "We haven't seen the long-neck rock yet, or the mountains that burn."

Cera was too excited to listen. She started down the ravine, with the others close behind. Suddenly there was a great rumble. The ground began to shake and they looked around in panic.

A huge herd of bump-heads was swooping down on the trees. It didn't take them long to pick the trees clean. Then they thundered away again.

Cera looked around angrily. "Look what those greedy bump-heads did!" she cried. "What happens to me now? I'm still hungry."

"You hungry?" Petrie whistled. "*I* empty all the way to my head! Now we at Great Valley and still not got green-foods."

But Littlefoot insisted that this wasn't the Great Valley.

"It is not a great anything," Ducky agreed. "Nope, nope."

Walking from tree to tree, the group found one that still had some leaves at the very top. It was too high for even Littlefoot to reach.

Then he got an idea. He had everyone form a pyramid, with Petrie at the top. But before they could get at the leaves, the pyramid collapsed, leaving Petrie and Ducky hanging from a single leaf.

A moment later the leaf tore, and Petrie and Ducky fell toward the ground, each still clutching half of the leaf. Littlefoot took a deep breath and blew upward. The leaf caught the air and Petrie and Ducky *floated* down.

In the next moment part of a branch that was full of tasty-looking green-food fell. Everyone dove into the feast—except Cera. She

stubbornly tried to get the rest of the branch down by butting the tree, but only made herself dizzy. Littlefoot felt sorry for her, and when she butted the tree once more, he threw a tuft of leaves into the air. It landed right next to her and she proudly looked around.

"See?" she said. "I can take care of *myself*." She went off and munched her food. "And I'm not afraid to be alone," she shouted. "I'm not afraid of Sharptooth. But I hope he doesn't eat any of you!"

The little group looked at each other anxiously.

"Don't worry," said Littlefoot. "There isn't any Sharptooth."

But that night, Petrie, Spike, and Ducky made sure they had plenty of company. First they snuggled near Cera. Then they snuggled near Littlefoot. In the middle of the night, when she was sure they were all asleep, Cera crept up to everyone else and snuggled in, too.

The next morning, as wisps of fog drifted by overhead, Cera woke up and sniffed the air. Something was out there in the gray mist. Then she looked down and realized that the large hole in which they had made their bed was really a giant footprint—Sharptooth's footprint!

"Wake up! Wake up, everybody!" she whispered loudly.

"Hey, stop that!" yelled Littlefoot. "I want to sleep."

A terrible and familiar roar suddenly shook the air. Through the fog the young travelers saw, to their horror, the huge shape of Sharptooth. And because of Littlefoot's yelling, he saw them, too! With another terrible cry, the big beast thundered toward them, his enormous mouth wide open and his one good eye glinting with hatred.

7 The Oasis

The group tried to run away, but Sharptooth was too quick. Whichever way they dodged, he cut them off.

"Run!" yelled Littlefoot. "I'll keep him busy!"

Petrie, on Littlefoot's head, was holding fast to the tree star. He was bug-eyed with terror. "We run, too!" he cried.

But Littlefoot was already trying to draw attention to himself. It worked—Sharptooth came after him and Petrie.

Cera darted into a small opening between some rocks, with Ducky and Spike close behind. Littlefoot and Petrie were only inches in front of the monster and could feel his hot breath on their necks.

"Now I wish I fly!" yelled Petrie as Littlefoot headed for the opening. Sharptooth took a vicious swipe at them. In panic, Petrie dropped the tree star, and Sharptooth crushed it with his massive feet.

Just as Littlefoot and Petrie squeezed between the rocks, Sharptooth plowed into the opening with tremendous force. But it was too small for him. He clawed at the entrance in a bellowing rage.

When the group huddled together again, Cera turned to Littlefoot and cried, "I told you Sharptooth was alive, you stupid long-neck! You nearly got us killed!"

"I'm sorry," said Littlefoot. "But we're safe now."

"Nobody's safe with you," said Cera. "It's a good thing *I* was around to save us."

"Brave Cera," cried Ducky. "You ran first to show us the way."

Cera wasn't sure what Ducky meant by that, but before she could answer, Littlefoot pointed and cried, "It's the rock that looks like a long-neck! That's the way to the Great Valley."

As the group trudged on they came to mountains that were smoking. Littlefoot said, "See? Those are the mountains that burn. We

are going the right way to the Great Valley for sure."

But the way through them was hard. Hot burning embers rained down on them from the erupting mountains, and they found themselves walking through deep ash. A long time passed, and the brave little group was getting more tired and hungry with each plodding step. At last they left the mountains behind. Now they were in a hot sandy desert.

"I tired," moaned Petrie. "Way to Great Valley too great way."

"We're almost there," cried Littlefoot. "Don't give up now."

Suddenly Spike became alert and sniffed the air.

"He must smell food," said Ducky. "It's the only thing that would wake him up."

Spike snorted and galloped over a small hill. The others followed, staring in wonder at what they saw. There was a small spring of water surrounded by a group of thin gray-noses. Near the spring but standing apart was a cluster of trees full of delicious-looking green-food, surrounded by a group of fat crown-heads.

Littlefoot and the others raced down the hill, yelling and cheering. But when they got closer, they saw the hard looks on everybody's face, and the cheers died in their throats.

A stern-looking gray-nose came up to them and said, "What do you want, little ones?"

"Food!" Littlefoot cried.

"And water, yep, yep," Ducky added.

A fat crown-head waddled up and said, "No food!"

"You may drink," said the gray-nose to Ducky. "You are a big-mouth like us. But," he continued, pointing to the rest of the group, "no water for them."

"But they need drinks, too!" Ducky protested. "They're my friends."

"These are your friends?" said the fat crown-head. "A three-horn? A long-neck, a spike-tail, and"—he pointed to Petrie—"and whatever *that* is."

"Yes, run away quickly," said the gray-nose to Ducky, "before spikes and horns grow on you."

Cera couldn't believe what she was hearing. She had never realized before how foolish it was to dislike someone just because he looked different. All she knew now was that they all needed food and water.

She reared up her head and said firmly, "We're hungry! All of us!"

The thin gray-nose stared at her. "And so are we," he finally said.

"Then why don't you share the water with the crown-heads?" said Littlefoot. "And they could share the food with you. Then you wouldn't be hungry and they wouldn't be thirsty."

"No, no, no," said the crown-head and the gray-nose at the same time.

"Well, if you don't change your minds, all of you will die," said Cera.

"Why don't you like each other anyway?" Ducky asked.

"The crown-heads are from the other side of the swamp," said the gray-nose.

"I don't see anything wrong with that," said Littlefoot.

"This is silly. I'm hungry," cried Cera. "Let's go somewhere else to look for food together."

And with that the small group marched away. The gray-nose shook his head. "I'll never understand the young ones," he said. The crown-head nodded and went back to guard the food.

A while later Littlefoot, Cera, and the rest of the group were at the bottom of a huge sandhill, panting with hunger and thirst. The brave words they had uttered before seemed to come back to mock them now. They were ready to give up—all but Littlefoot. "After what we've been through together, you can't quit now," he pleaded.

"Ahhh," Petrie whistled. "Good time to quit."

"Yes, it is too hard, too far. I cannot go to the Great Valley. Nope, nope, nope," Ducky said, sighing.

"But what if the Great Valley is just over the top of this hill?" said Littlefoot.

"What if the Great Valley is nowhere?" cried Cera. "I've never seen it. Have you?"

"I've seen it with my heart," answered Littlefoot. And he started to climb up the hill. The others shrugged and followed wearily.

"You see? I told you, you stupid flathead," said Cera when they had reached the top. "There's nothing but a big crater here." She was about to go back down the hill, but the sand underneath her suddenly gave way, and she and the others slid to the bottom of the rocky crater.

When they shakily got to their feet and looked around, they saw two distant paths leading out of the crater. One sloped gently through a notch in the crater wall. The other was a narrow trail straight up that looked hard and dangerous to climb.

Littlefoot headed for the narrow trail. "This way," he yelled.

But Cera didn't want to take the hard path. She saw other animals' footprints going up the easy path, and she wanted to take it.

"But we have to keep on following the bright circle. There, up that narrow trail," said Littlefoot.

"Well, you go up there, then," Cera said angrily. Ducky and Spike followed Cera, leaving Petrie alone with Littlefoot.

"I think maybe time to go new way," Petrie whistled.

Littlefoot angrily tossed Petrie off his head. "You're the flier," he shouted. "Fly off and find the valley yourself....I don't need you. I don't need any of you!" He turned in the direction of the bright circle and the hard path. Ducky, Petrie, and Spike waved a tearful good-bye and turned to follow Cera.

8 Danger Everywhere

Cera led the group up the easy path out of the crater. Now the going was anything but easy. All about them burning mountains were spewing fire and smoke. Red fog swirled around them, reflecting the sides of the mountains. Everywhere they looked were black caves and dark ravines, and they imagined all sorts of creatures lurking within them.

Now, too, they could see what had happened to the other animals that had come this way. Skeletons and bodies of dead animals loomed out of the mist and seemed to be warning them to go back.

"I wish Littlefoot were with us now," whispered Ducky.

Spike nodded in agreement as he stopped to nibble at a scrawny bush.

"Spike! Do not stop!" cried Ducky. "Nope, nope! We must stay together. We do not want to be alone...*do* we?" But even as she said that, she noticed they *were* alone. Cera and Petrie had disappeared into the misty fog.

Meanwhile, Littlefoot had just climbed out of the crater and faced

a lonely plain. He looked around forlornly, hardly able to move. Just then something in the sky caught his attention. It was a large cloud that took on a familiar shape.

"Mother?" he whispered with a lump in his throat.

He felt a gentle wind caress his face. It seemed to be whispering to him. "Littlefoot..." It was his mother's voice!

"I tried to do what you told me, Mother. But it's just too hard. I can't hear my heart. I'll never find the Great Valley." The cloud vision began to drift away. "Mother! Don't go," he cried.

He chased after the cloud across the wide plain as the wind whispered around him. The sound seemed to be rising and falling like

a melody, and then suddenly he heard singing! He wondered if he was imagining it, but no—there it was again, a high, sweet song carried along by the breeze. Below the cloud, he saw an opening into a beautiful green valley—the Great Valley.

His heart swelling with joy, Littlefoot started to race down into the wonderful valley. But then he heard his mother's voice again in the wind. "Littlefoot…"

He skidded to a stop. In his heart he knew what his mother was going to tell him. "The others…they went the wrong way! They'll never find the Great Valley!" He looked up at the cloud. The image of his mother was fading.

"Mother! What should I do?" he asked. But he answered himself. "My heart…my heart says…they're my friends! I have to help them!"

With that, he turned and raced out of the valley.

"Cera knows right way to go? Real sure?" Petrie asked as he rode along on her head.

"Of course I do," answered Cera impatiently.

"I scared," Petrie whistled.

"Well I'm not scared," said Cera stubbornly.

"I wonder if Littlefoot lonesome?" Petrie said.

"I don't care if that long-neck is lonesome," she said.

Petrie was about to answer her when a low-hanging branch knocked him right off Cera's head. He didn't even have time to whistle before he found himself in a sticky tar pit. He yelled for Cera. But she had gone on, not realizing that he wasn't with her anymore. He looked behind him for Spike and Ducky, but they weren't there either. The more he struggled to get free of the tar, the deeper he sank.

In the meantime, Littlefoot was rushing through the dark scary landscape. He could see only by the light of the fire-rivers and the flames from the burning mountains.

He craned his neck this way and that and frantically called out. All of a sudden he stopped in his tracks at the edge of a sharp cliff. A smoking mountain spewing a fire-river towered above him. And below were Ducky and Spike, trapped on a rock in a red glowing fire-river.

He raced down across the hot rocks toward them. The bit of rock on which they stood was quickly falling apart. With his strong neck he pushed a large rock into the fiery liquid next to Ducky and Spike's rock. It formed a bridge between them and solid ground. Ducky and Spike jumped across to safety just as their rock disappeared into the bubbling red river with a loud hiss.

From somewhere up ahead they heard a faint cry. It was Petrie!

When they reached him, only his beak and frightened eyes showed above the tar.

The group quickly decided on a plan of action. Littlefoot wrapped his strong tail around a huge dead tree near the pit. He clamped his mouth around Spike's tail, and Spike waded out to try to reach Petrie. But the little flier was just out of reach. So Ducky ran along Littlefoot's back and then onto Spike's head. She could just reach Petrie. With one good pull, she yanked him up and onto Spike's head.

As three of them cheered, the dead tree snapped in two. Now they were all sinking into the gooey mess. Struggling to get free, they suddenly heard Cera scream from somewhere nearby.

"You get away! Stay away!" she cried.

"Cera needs help!" Littlefoot yelled.

"We all need help," whistled Petrie as they sank into the tar pit.

Cera had found herself trapped in a dark cave, surrounded by four lizard-heads. They circled her and hissed viciously. One of them lunged at her, but she bravely reared back and spit in its face.

"Get away, you mean lizard-heads!" she cried as she scrambled up some rocks. But the lizard-heads wouldn't give up. Cera hopped around, hoping to make a break for the mouth of the cave, but the lizard-heads were closing in fast. It looked like the end.

"Aaaaargggh!" A tremendous echoing roar came from the mouth of the cave. As the lizard-heads looked back in surprise, a huge ugly black beast towered over them. The beast roared again and lifted Cera by the tail, holding her upside down. The lizard-heads didn't wait to see what would happen next. But now Cera had a new monster to face.

She hung there terrified. Oh, if only her friends were here! It was in that moment of danger that she realized that they *were* her friends.

"Help me!" she screamed. "Spike! Ducky! Petrie!"

Then the big monster spoke. "Cera! It's us!" it said.

Cera twirled around upside down and saw the monster close-up. It really was Littlefoot, Petrie, Ducky, and Spike—all stuck together with tar!

At first she was relieved, but then she was mad. She had shown that she needed and wanted them. And she didn't want to do that. Her pride was still controlling her heart.

"I knew it was you all along!" she said.

Littlefoot grinned at her.

"You did?" said Ducky. "But you were screaming so loud."

"I was only acting," Cera shot back. "I wanted those scaly-skins to come into the cave so I could attack *them*!"

"Nope, nope, nope," Ducky said, shaking her head.

"Oh, get out of my way!" Cera yelled. But as she tried to stalk out of the cave, she stuck to the tar monster.

"We really together now!" said Ducky, giggling.

"Yeah, Cera," said Littlefoot. "Now we have to stick together." And the whole group laughed.

That made Cera madder than ever. Pulling herself free, she cried out, "Oh, shut up. I hate all of you! I don't ever want to see any of you again, ever!"

With that, she stomped out of the cave into the darkness. As she marched away her eyes filled with tears. She really didn't mean what she had said. It was just that her pride had been hurt. She looked

around, half expecting them to come after her. But they didn't, and her heart sank a little.

A heavy rain started to fall, washing the tar off Littlefoot and the others. "Let her go," he said. "If she doesn't want to come back, there's nothing we can do." The others sadly had to agree.

The next morning Littlefoot, Ducky, Spike, and Petrie headed down the path toward the Great Valley.

"We're almost there," said Littlefoot. "Just a little farther."

"Too bad Cera not with us," said Petrie.

As the group rounded a pool near the cliffs by the entrance to the valley, Petrie leapt off Littlefoot's head and climbed to a high, rocky ledge. Suddenly be began to quiver with fear.

"Petrie, what is it?" Littlefoot asked as he reached the ledge. Then he looked beyond it. There, on the plain that overlooked the Great Valley, was Sharptooth. He was searching for the entrance to the valley!

9 The Great Valley

Littlefoot realized that they had led Sharptooth to the valley. He knew that the herds would be helpless against the monster. He and his friends had to stop Sharptooth.

Littlefoot noticed a large boulder balanced at the edge of a rock ledge high above a pool of water. "We've got to get Sharptooth away from the high rocks before he finds the entrance," he said to the others. "And then we'll have to work together to kill him."

"How?" asked Petrie.

"We'll coax him to the deep end of the pond here. He can't swim with those scrawny arms," Littlefoot said. "Spike and I will go up to that rock. We'll push it off onto his head. He'll fall over into the water."

"Oh, he will be mad, he will," Ducky said, worried.

Littlefoot turned to Petrie. "Petrie," he said, "you be the lookout and whistle when he's in just the right spot. Where the water gets dark is the deepest part."

Then he turned to Ducky. "We need someone to be the bait."

"Me? Oh, no....Nope, nope, nope!" cried Ducky.

A short time later Sharptooth found the entrance to the Great Valley. He growled and sniffed the air with evil joy. Just then, a noise behind him caught his attention. Roaring, he whipped around and saw a little big-mouth heading for a pool of water. She looked injured. He grunted in satisfaction at the juicy little morsel just waiting to be eaten! He pounded after her with a raging bellow.

Ducky's heart was beating faster than it ever had before. She knew that Littlefoot and Spike were near the big rock, getting ready to push, and that Petrie was hidden in a crevice above, ready to tell them when. But that didn't stop her legs from trembling. Behind her, Sharptooth was fast approaching.

"Faster, Ducky," she said to herself. "Real fast, yep, yep, yep."

She splashed into the pool and quickly swam out to the center. Sharptooth followed close behind, sending up huge sprays of water. Ducky kept on swimming until she was in the deepest part of the pool. Sharptooth closed in on her. Then a shrill whistle caught his attention. It was Petrie signaling.

Up above, Littlefoot and Spike were frantically trying to push the rock over onto Sharptooth, but it wouldn't budge. Now Sharptooth went after Petrie. He clawed at the rock wall, sending big chunks of rock splashing into the pool. Sharptooth's attack was weakening the ledge that Petrie was perched on. Suddenly it gave way and he plunged down into Sharptooth's waiting jaws.

The little flier flapped his wings in frantic fear, but he kept falling.

Just as he reached Sharptooth's gnashing jaws, he suddenly felt himself rising. He was flying!

Sharptooth roared in anger at Petrie's escape and turned to go after Ducky once more. Petrie felt braver now that he could fly, and with a whistle of joy he zoomed down and pecked hard at Sharptooth's head. Sharptooth snapped his jaws and swiped angrily as Petrie circled and zoomed down to peck at him again.

Littlefoot screamed from above, "Get him over the deep part, Petrie!" But Sharptooth ignored Petrie and went after Ducky again. As he opened his jaws for the kill, Ducky saw rows and rows of sharp teeth.

Petrie saw what was happening and he whistled in fury as he once more zoomed at Sharptooth, landing on his head. He put one wing over Sharptooth's good eye and held on for dear life. Sharptooth reeled around in anger as he tried to get the maddening little creature off his face. He butted his head and rubbed it along the rocks. Petrie looked up and saw that Sharptooth was right underneath the rock.

"Push rock now!" he whistled.

"Yep, now!" cried Ducky.

But Littlefoot and Spike still couldn't push the rock over. Petrie was getting tired holding on to Sharptooth's face, and his wing fell away from the monster's eye. Now that he could see what he was doing, Sharptooth roared in rage and charged at the rock wall—and Petrie. As Petrie screamed—someone else did, too.

From out of nowhere, Cera appeared. As Littlefoot and Spike pushed with all their might, Cera let out her battle cry and charged at the rock. It went tumbling over and landed with a loud thud right on Sharptooth's head. With a tremendous splash the great beast sank into the deep part of the pool and disappeared. Littlefoot and his friends smiled at each other in awe and satisfaction. They had done it—but only as a team.

Littlefoot's smile quickly turned into a worried look. "Where's Petrie?" he asked.

"Poor, poor Petrie," said Ducky, and everyone felt very sad.

After a long silence, Littlefoot said, "Petrie was a good friend. He would want us to continue…come." And he led the little group away from the pool and toward the Great Valley. Just then they heard a cough and a sigh and turned to see a soggy Petrie pulling himself onto the rocks.

"Petrie…you're safe!" screamed Ducky. "Yep, yep, yep."

And at that moment everyone, even Cera, hugged each other in joy and friendship.

"Now we'll always be together," cried Littlefoot.

"How long?" whistled Petrie.

"Forever!" Ducky cried.

"Together," said Cera, a broad smile on her face.

"Come on!" yelled Littlefoot. "We've waited long enough. Let's go to the Great Valley."

A short while later they found themselves at the entrance to the valley. The view was so breathtaking that they stopped and gaped in disbelief.

Rich-looking trees were everywhere, bursting with so much green-food that they looked as if they might topple with the weight. Thick emerald grass covered the ground as far as the eye could see. And there were rivers and pools of fresh clear water. All the herds were there—big-mouths, long-necks, three-horns—living side by side peacefully.

As they watched, they heard a beautiful song coming from the valley. As the song grew louder, they rushed into the valley, shouting with joy.

It wasn't long before they all found their families again, except for Spike. But he was quickly adopted by Ducky's family when she explained that he was her friend forever, yep, yep. Cera, Littlefoot, Spike, Ducky, and Petrie vowed that there would be no differences between them ever again. They would teach the adults what they had learned.

Later, as Littlefoot stood alone on top of a windy hill overlooking the valley, he gazed up at the sky. For a moment the clouds blew into a familiar shape, and he seemed to hear his mother's voice again.

"You have learned to follow your heart," it whispered. "Good-bye, Littlefoot. Don't forget me."

"Good-bye, Mother," whispered Littlefoot. "I won't forget you. You will be in my heart forever."

He looked out at the Great Valley once more and then went down the hill to join his family and friends. And as he did, he could hear his heart singing.

ANDOZALAVDHARBYBY.
AVRAFDR

AND ZAT ASTheAND